E HALL, W
Hall, Wendy J.,
Carter's CT scan /

Wendy J Hall
Visit the website at
https://www.mediwonderland.com/

First Printing: October 2017
Mediwonderland

ISBN-13: 978-1722950941

Carter's CT Scan

Wendy J. Hall

In the middle of the night, Carter woke up with terrible pains in his tummy. It hurt so much that he couldn't stand up straight.

He moaned and groaned in pain until his mom woke up.

She rushed into his room to find out what the matter was.

"What's the matter, Carter?" asked his mom.

"My tummy is really hurting," he sobbed, holding it.

"Oh dear!" said his mom. "We'd better go and get you checked out at the hospital.

"I wonder if you ate something that upset your tummy," she said.

When they got to the hospital, they were very relieved to see Dr. Daniel, their favorite doctor. He was on night duty.

"What can I do for you? You look like you're in terrible pain."

"My tummy really hurts here," said Carter, pointing to a part of his tummy.

"Let's have you up on the examination table so I can take a look."

Nurse Nina helped him up onto the table.

"I'm sorry but I need to push down on your tummy and you need to tell me when it hurts," Dr. Daniel told him. "I will be as gentle as possible."

He started to push down on Carter's tummy in different places. Each time, Carter shrieked, "Ouch!"

"I don't think it is anything serious but we need to take a look inside!"

"How can we do that?" asked Carter, feeling better now that Nurse Nina had given him some medicine to help take the pain away.

"I am going to send you for a special scan called a CT scan."

"A CT scan?" said Carter.

"I can see that you're feeling better," said Dr. Daniel. "A CT scan is a special kind of X-ray test that takes pictures of your body so we can see your insides clearly.

"Nurse Nina will explain all about it and get you ready for it now. You need to get changed into a special gown."

Nurse Nina helped Carter tie the back of the gown. Then she told him that a CT scan machine looks like a big, round donut.

"You just have to lie very still on the table, which will move in and out of the 'donut' part."

Carter felt curious and even excited about going inside the "donut."

"There is one thing I have to tell you though. So the technician (sometimes called technologist) can get a good picture, something called 'contrast' will need to be injected into your veins.

"It's a dye that shows up on the pictures and will help Dr. Daniel see more clearly."

"How will it get into my veins?" asked Carter, who was starting to feel nervous.

"I'm going to put a special needle into your hand and then the contrast will travel through that. It will hurt for a few seconds while I put the needle in but I promise I'm very gentle and I know you are very brave!"

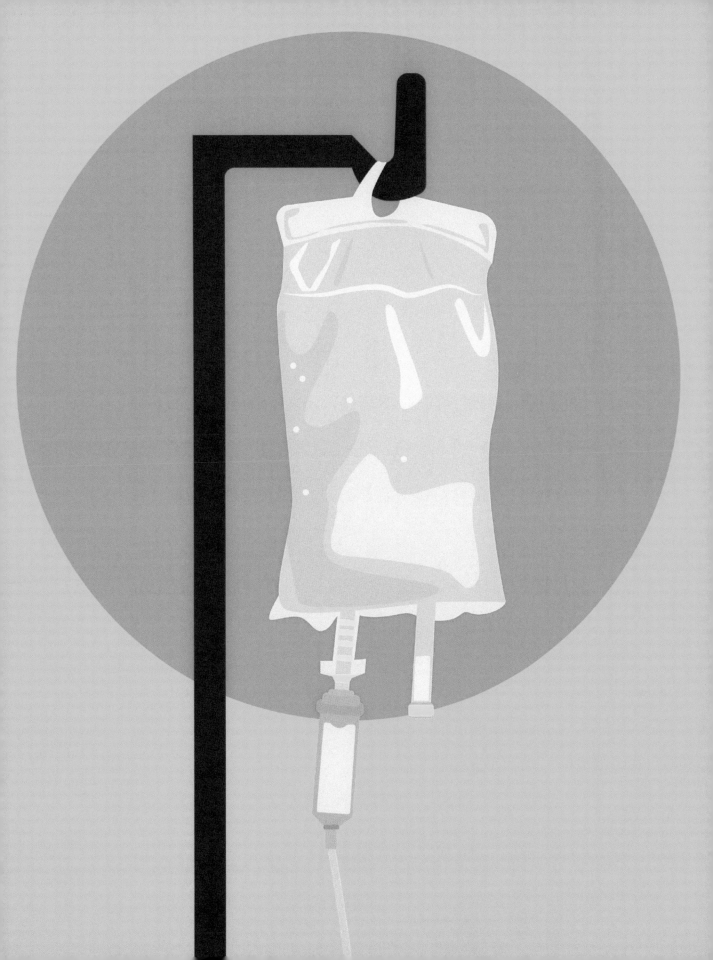

Carter tried to be brave while Nurse Nina put a needle into his hand with a little plastic stopper on. Then she used a syringe to push some water through it and into his vein.

It felt cold as it went up his arm, and he chuckled.

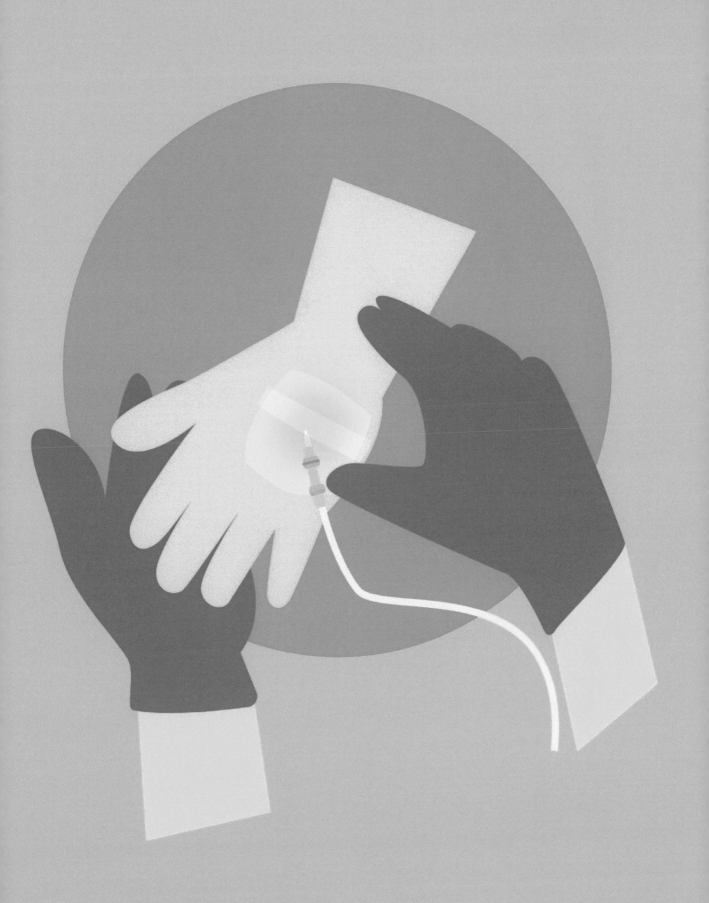

"There you go! You're all fixed now, but first I need to tell you a secret. When the technician puts the contrast liquid into your vein, you will feel a strange warm feeling and then you will feel like you have wet yourself but you won't have!"

Carter laughed at the thought of that.

Soon, Carter was lying on the table and, sure enough, it looked like a huge donut. The technician asked him to lie very still and listen to her instructions.

When the contrast went into his vein, he got a warm feeling but Nurse Nina had prepared him well for it.

It did feel funny and warm.

An hour later, they were back in Dr. Daniel's office.

"I know why you had terrible tummy pain. Has it been a long time since you last went to the toilet? There is a lot of poop in your bowel and it got blown up, causing you pain. We call it 'constipation.' This is a picture of your tummy and this is your large intestine where all your poop is stuck.

"It's not serious. We just need to fix your diet and you'll soon be better again."

Digestive System

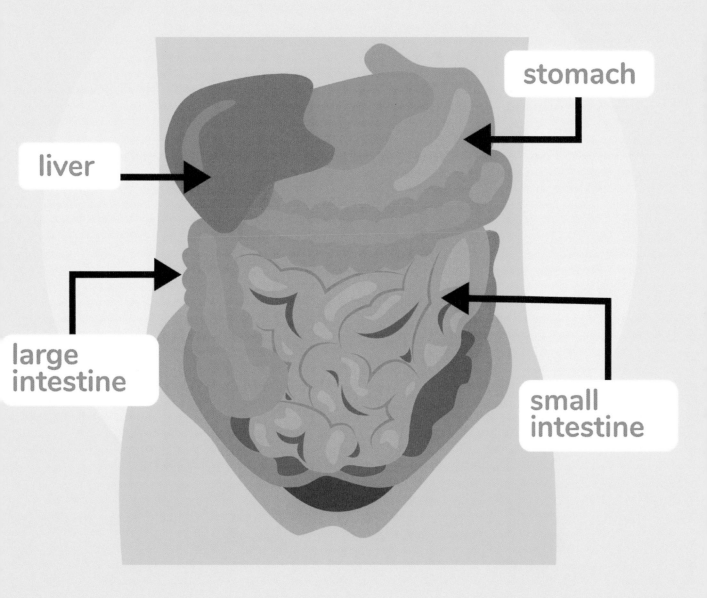

stomach

liver

large intestine

small intestine

He gave Carter's mom some medicine for Carter.

He also told Carter that he needed to eat more fruit, vegetables and food containing fiber. He also reminded him to drink more water.

Finally, he gave Carter's mom an information leaflet. They left happily, knowing that Carter would be OK.

The next day at school, Carter told his friends about his adventure in a "donut" machine.

About the Author

Originally from the UK, Wendy speaks five languages and has authored over 100 educational books. The inspiration for this innovative series comes from personal experience: Her own daughter, then aged eight, once spent a year in hospital and underwent major surgery.

While taking care of a scared child, Wendy could not find materials that helped her navigate the healthcare system. This situation kindled a dream: to provide parents and medical professionals with a tool to make medical procedures, illnesses, and adverse childhood circumstances less frightening.

Wendy has extensive knowledge of the medical field as she herself suffers from a rare, chronic illness. An award-winning Patient Leader, she works to improve healthcare by advocating and educating.

To learn more about Wendy, please visit the website:

https://www.mediwonderland.com

Made in the USA
Monee, IL
25 September 2019